# Dreams Are Made for Children

## Classic Jazz Lullabies

# Lullaby of Birdland

Singer **Sarah Vaughan** Words **George Weiss** Music **George Shearing**

Lullaby of birdland
That's what I always hear, when you sigh
Never in my wordland could there be ways to reveal
In a phrase how I feel

Have you ever heard two turtle doves
Bill and coo when they love?
That's the kind of magic music we make
With our lips, when we kiss

And there's a weepy old willow
He really knows how to cry
That's how I cry in my pillow
If you should tell me farewell and goodbye

Lullaby of birdland, whisper low
Kiss me sweet and we'll go
Flying high in birdland, high in the sky up above
All because we're in love

Sarah Vaughan's extraordinary range and masterful vocal technique made her the most complete and remarkable singer in modern jazz. This perfect rendition of "Lullaby of Birdland" shows off her improvisational skill, her facility with scat and her incredible voice, which she seems to play as though it were an instrument.

# Lullaby in Blue

Singers **Debbie Reynolds** and **Eddie Fisher** Words **Adam Cohen** Music **Brock Walsh**

**Hushaby, rockaby**
**Listen to my lullaby in blue**
**How I love my pretty baby**
**Sweet and precious pretty baby**
**How I love my pretty baby**
**Honest to goodness I do**

**See here, sandman's coming**
**And he'll be here mighty, mighty soon**
**And if you don't cry**
**You'll be dropping by**
**With a great big lollypop moon**

**Dream, dream, dream**
**Be an angel**
**Dream, dream, dream**
**Be a darling**
**I love my pretty baby**
**Honest to goodness I do**

Like many jazz standards, this lullaby sung by Debbie Reynolds and Eddie Fisher (husband and wife at the time) was introduced in a film musical, in this case *Bundle of Joy* released in 1956. The story is about an unmarried salesgirl in a department store who finds an abandoned baby and decides to take care of it. All kinds of hilarious confusion ensues.

# Dreams Are Made for Children

Singer **Ella Fitzgerald** Words and music **Mack David, Jerry Livingston** and **Max Meth**

Dim the light, little man
And tonight, little man
On a ship of dreams you'll sail

Dreams are made for children
And a dream is a fairytale

You don't need a magic wand
To see all that lies beyond
If you just believe in fairyland
Fairyland appears

Dream away, little man
Dream as long as you can
Don't grow up, I beg of you

Dreams are made for children
And for children dreams come true

Ella Fitzgerald was one of the greatest jazz singers of all time. Her pure voice, three-octave range and superb vocal agility were matched by a rare talent for improvisation, especially when it came to scat. She had a melodic style that was right at home in any tempo or type of repertoire. One of Ella Fitzgerald's most memorable improvisations came during a 1960 concert in Berlin. She was singing Kurt Weill's "Mack the Knife" from The Three Penny Opera when she forgot the words. But she never missed a beat as she kept right on with a mixture of scat and improvised lyrics. This lullaby was made famous in 1958 by Shirley Temple on her television show, *Shirley Temple's Storybook.*

# My Sleepy Head (Go to Sleep)

Singer **Nat King Cole** Words and music **Larry Coleman** and **Paul Secon**

Little one, put your toys away
You had fun playing games all day
Time for bed
Go to sleep my sleepy head

Soon you'll find candy dreams and such
On your mind
If you eat too much
I won't mind
Go to sleep my sleepy head

Away to dreamland
That grand man the sandman
Will lead you
And may an angel be there beside you
There to guide you through the night

Time to pray
Lay me down to sleep
Now you say
And my soul to keep

Time for bed
Go to sleep my sleepy head
Good night

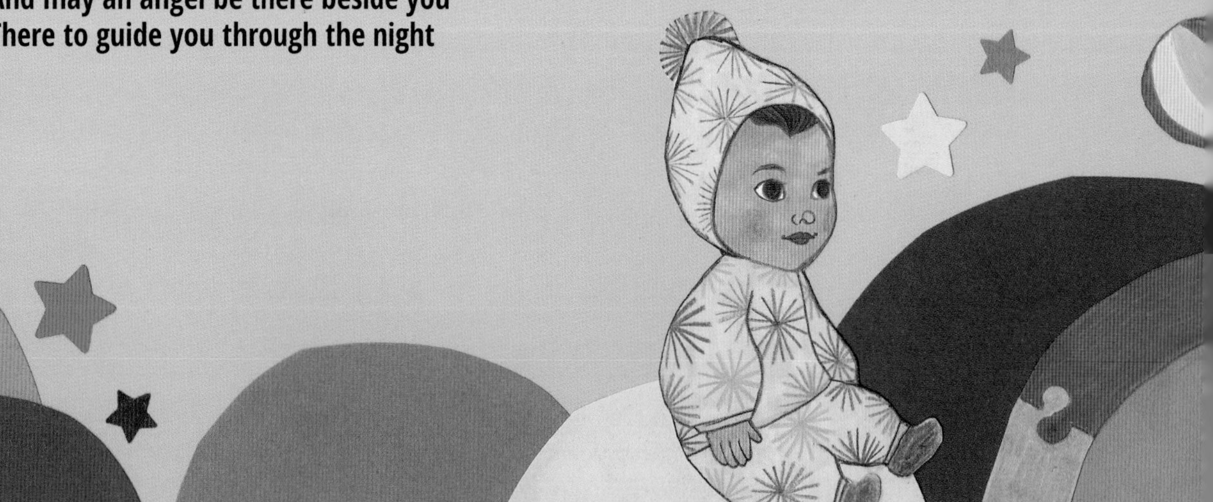

Nat King Cole had a wonderfully gentle, deep voice and played the piano with a subtle, nervous swing combined with great rhythmic precision. His ability to perform in styles ranging from standards to Broadway hits and Latin American songs made him a popular favourite with the public. He also set a precedent in jazz by forming a trio that featured a guitar-piano combo up front.

# Over the Rainbow

**Singer** Judy Garland **Words** E. Y. Harburg **Music** Harold Arlen

Somewhere, over the rainbow
Way up high
There's a land that I heard of
Once in a lullaby

Somewhere, over the rainbow
Skies are blue
And the dreams that you dare to dream
Really do come true

Someday I'll wish upon a star and wake up
Where the clouds are far behind me
Where troubles melt like lemon drops
Away above the chimney tops
That's where you'll find me

Somewhere, over the rainbow
Blue birds fly
Birds fly over the rainbow
Why, oh, why can't I?

If happy little bluebirds fly
Beyond the rainbow
Why, oh, why can't I?

Written in 1900 by L. Frank Baum, the children's novel *The Wizard of Oz* became a classic of American literature. In 1939, it was made into a film directed by Victor Fleming and starring Judy Garland in the role of Dorothy, for which she won a special Academy Award for Best Performance by a Juvenile. The film is particularly remembered for its songs, especially "Over the Rainbow," whose popularity has never waned.

# Goodnight My Love

**Singer** Sarah Vaughan **Words** Mack Gordon **Music** Harry Revel

Goodnight my love
The tired old moon is descending
Goodnight my love
My moment with you now is ending
It was so heavenly
Holding you close to me
It will be heavenly
To hold you again in a dream
The stars above
Have promised to meet us tomorrow
Till then, my love
How dreary the new day will seem
So for the present, dear
We'll have to part
Sleep tight my love
Goodnight my love
Remember that you're mine, sweetheart

Goodnight my love
Your little Dutch dolly is yawning
Goodnight my love
Your teddy bear called it a day
Your doggy's fast asleep
My, but he's smart
Sleep tight my love
Goodnight my love
God bless you
Pleasant dreams, sweetheart

This popular song appeared for the first time in the 1936 musical film *Stowaway*, performed by Shirley Temple—just eight years old at the time—and Alice Faye. Sarah Vaughan turns "Goodnight My Love" into a sweet and sensual love song.

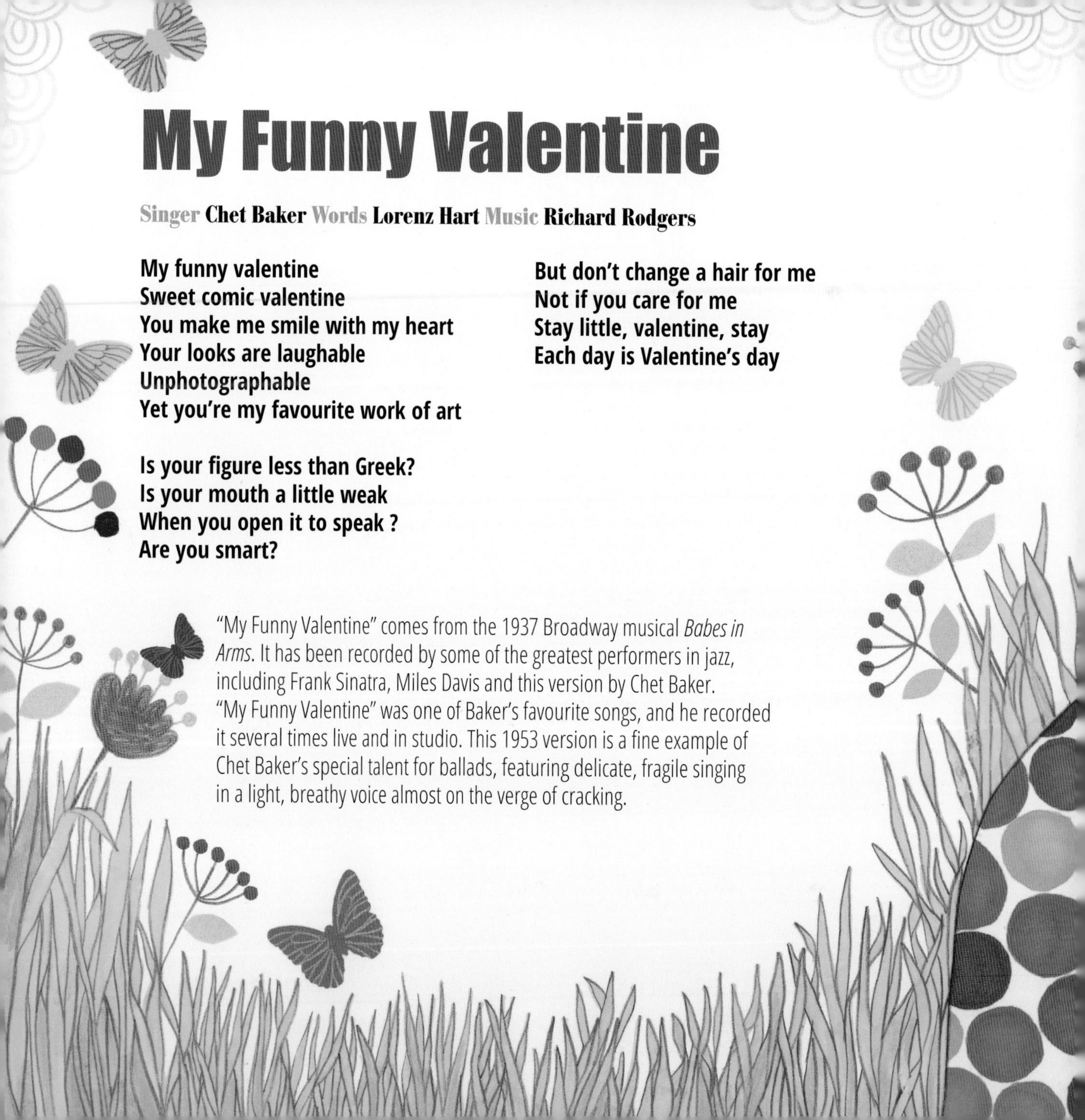

# My Funny Valentine

Singer **Chet Baker** Words **Lorenz Hart** Music **Richard Rodgers**

**My funny valentine**
**Sweet comic valentine**
**You make me smile with my heart**
**Your looks are laughable**
**Unphotographable**
**Yet you're my favourite work of art**

**Is your figure less than Greek?**
**Is your mouth a little weak**
**When you open it to speak ?**
**Are you smart?**

**But don't change a hair for me**
**Not if you care for me**
**Stay little, valentine, stay**
**Each day is Valentine's day**

"My Funny Valentine" comes from the 1937 Broadway musical *Babes in Arms*. It has been recorded by some of the greatest performers in jazz, including Frank Sinatra, Miles Davis and this version by Chet Baker. "My Funny Valentine" was one of Baker's favourite songs, and he recorded it several times live and in studio. This 1953 version is a fine example of Chet Baker's special talent for ballads, featuring delicate, fragile singing in a light, breathy voice almost on the verge of cracking.

# Hit the Road to Dreamland

Singer **Mel Tormé** Words and music **Harold Harlem** and **John Herndon Mercer**

**Bye bye baby**
**Time to hit the road to Dreamland**
**You're my baby**
**Dig you in the land of nod**

**Hold tight baby**
**We'll be swinging up in Dreamland**
**All night baby**
**Where the little cherubs trot**

**Look at that knocked out moon**
**You been a-blowing his top in the blue**
**Never saw the likes of you**
**What an angel**

**Bye bye baby**
**Time to hit the road to Dreamland**
**Don't cry baby**
**It was divine**
**But the rooster has finally crowed**
**Time to hit the road**

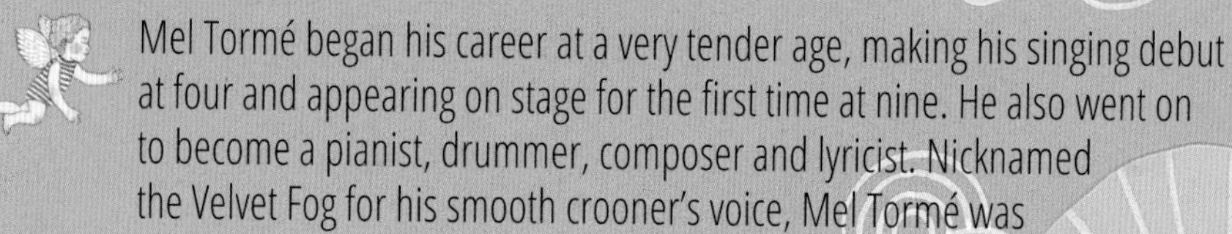

Mel Tormé began his career at a very tender age, making his singing debut at four and appearing on stage for the first time at nine. He also went on to become a pianist, drummer, composer and lyricist. Nicknamed the Velvet Fog for his smooth crooner's voice, Mel Tormé was an integral part of the world of jazz and its musicians.

# Summertime

**Singer Peggy Lee Words and music Ira and George Gershwin**

Summertime, living's easy
Summertime, and the living is easy
Fish are jumping
And the cotton is high

Oh, your daddy's rich
And your ma is good looking
So, hush little baby
Don't you cry

One of these mornings
You're gonna rise up singing
Then you'll spread your wings
And you'll take to the sky

But until that morning
There's nothing can harm you
With daddy and mammy standing by
Summertime

Peggy Lee was a singer and all-round musician. She performed with great depth of feeling, phrased beautifully and had a remarkable sense of rhythm. Her uniquely deep, warm voice set her apart from similar artists. She wrote the lyrics and music for many hit songs, including the title song for Disney's *Lady and the Tramp.* George Gershwin's younger brother Ira penned the words to "Summertime" and several other great hits of the twentieth-century, including "I Got Rhythm," "The Man I Love" and the folk opera *Porgy and Bess,* from which "Summertime" comes. The many versions recorded of this song include a wonderful and beloved duet by Louis Armstrong and Ella Fitzgerald.

# Looking For A Boy

Singer **Chris Connor** Words and music **Ira** and **George Gershwin**

If it's true that love affairs
Are all arranged in heaven
My guardian angel's holding out on me
So I'm looking for a boy
'Bout five foot six or seven
And won't be happy till I'm on his knee
I'll be blue until he comes my way
Hope he takes the cue
When I am saying:

I am just a little girl
Who's looking for a little boy
Who's looking for a girl to love
Tell me please, where can he be
The loving he who'll bring to me
The harmony I'm dreaming of?

It would be goodbye, I know
To my tale of woe
When he says hello, so
I am just a little girl
Who's looking for a little boy
Who's looking for a girl to love

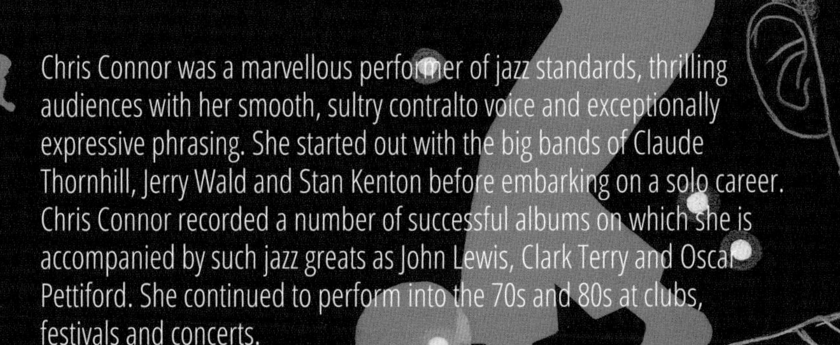

Chris Connor was a marvellous performer of jazz standards, thrilling audiences with her smooth, sultry contralto voice and exceptionally expressive phrasing. She started out with the big bands of Claude Thornhill, Jerry Wald and Stan Kenton before embarking on a solo career. Chris Connor recorded a number of successful albums on which she is accompanied by such jazz greats as John Lewis, Clark Terry and Oscar Pettiford. She continued to perform into the 70s and 80s at clubs, festivals and concerts.

# God Bless the Child

**Singer** Billie Holiday **Words** Arthur Herzoz **Music** Eleonara MacKay

Them that's got shall get
Them that's not shall lose
So the Bible said and it still is news
Mama may have, Papa may have
But God bless the child that's got his own

Yes the strong get more
While the weak ones fade
Empty pockets don't ever make the grade
Mama may have, Papa may have
But God bless the child that's got his own

Money, you've got lots of friends
Crowding round the door
When you're gone and spending ends
They don't come no more
Rich relations give
Crusts of bread and such
You can help yourself
But don't take too much
Mama may have, Papa may have
But God bless the child that's got his own

Mama may have, Papa may have
But God bless the child that's got his own
He just don't worry about nothing
Cause he's got his own

Nicknamed Lady Day by saxophonist Lester Young, Billie Holiday is considered one of the greatest singers jazz has ever known. Her voice was raspy and sensual with a touch of vibrato. Although her articulation tended to drag, she possessed a unique sense of rhythm, holding back almost imperceptibly and using a relaxed phrasing to create her own unique style of swing. She pushed expression to the limit without ever making the performance about her voice or technique and used raw emotion fed by her tumultuous past to bring original compositions and jazz standards to life.

# Brahm's Lullaby

Singer **Frank Sinatra**

**Lullaby and good night**
**With roses delight**
**Bright angels around my darling shall stay**
**Lady down now and rest**
**May thy slumber be blest**

Frank Sinatra was an internationally renowned crooner, known simply as "The Voice." His close association with the world of jazz arose not only from his choice of arrangers (such as Johnny Mandel and Quincy Jones) and orchestra leaders (including Count Bassie, Duke Ellington and Buddy Rich) but also from his singing style, marked by swing, an easy style at any tempo from upbeat to slow ballad, risk-taking and rich phrasing. Frank Sinatra sold more than 150 million albums around the world.

## Music publishing and master recording credits

### Lullaby of Birdland

Singer **Sarah Vaughan** Words **George Weiss**
Music **George Shearing**

© EMI Longitude Music Avec © 1957, Mercury

### Lullaby in Blue

Singers **Debbie Reynolds** and **Eddie Fisher**
Words **Adam Cohen** Music **Brock Walsh**

© Cabesaluna Music administered by Wixen Music, Universal Polygram International and Very Little Grey Music administered by Universal Polygram International © 1957, RCA

### Dreams Are Made for Children

Singer **Ella Fitzgerald** Words and music **Mack David, Jerry Livingston** and **Max Meth**

© Warner Bros. Inc. and Universal Polygram International © 1958

### My Sleepy Head (Go to Sleep)

Singer **Nat King Cole** Words and music by **Larry Coleman** and **Paul Secon**

© Warner Bros. Inc. © 1947, Capitol

### Over the Rainbow

Singer **Judy Garland** Words **E. Y. Harburg**
Music **Harold Arlen**

© EMI Feist Catalog Inc. © 1939, MGM

### Goodnight My Love

Singer **Sarah Vaughan** Words **Mack Gordon**
Music **Harry Revel**

© Ole Grand Films administered by EMI Music Publishing Inc. © 1950, Columbia

## My Funny Valentine

Singer **Chet Baker** Words **Lorenz Hart**
Music **Richard Rodgers**



## Hit the Road to Dreamland

Singer **Mel Tormé** Words and music **Harold Harlem** and **John Herndon Mercer**



## Summertime

Singer **Peggy Lee** Words and music **George Gershwin, DuBose** and **Dorothy Heyward, Ira Gershwin**



## Looking For A Boy

Singer **Chris Connor**
Words and music **Ira and George Gershwin**



## God Bless the Child

Singer **Billie Holiday** Words **Arthur Herzoz**
Music **Eleonara MacKay**

Song selection **Misja Fitzgerald Michel** Illustrations **Ilya Green**
Editing, mixing and mastering **Sébastien Noly (Studio Sonogramme)**
Graphic Design **Célestin Forestier and Stephan Lorti (Haus Design)**
Copy editing **Ruth Joseph** Translation **David Lytle and Hélène Roulston (Service d'édition Guy Connolly)**

Aknowledgements Bibliothéque nationale de France (Audio-Visual Department) www.thesecretmountain.com
 • ISBN 10: 2-924217-68-7 / ISBN 13: 978-2-924217-68-9
First published in France by Didier Jeunesse, Paris, 2012


Printed in Hong Kong by Book Art Inc. (Toronto).